IF AT FIRST YOU DO NOT SEE

For Ken

First published in the United States in 1983 by
Henry Holt and Company, Inc.,
115 West 18th Street,
New York, New York 10011.
Published in Canada by Fitzhenry & Whiteside Limited,
195 Allstate Parkway, Markham, Ontario L3R 4T8.
Originally published in Great Britain by Andersen Press Ltd.

Library of Congress Cataloging in Publication Data
Brown, Ruth.
If at first you do not see.
Summary: A caterpillar has some scary adventures before becoming
a beautiful butterfly. The reader needs to turn the book as he reads,
as there is writing around the sides of the pages.
[1. Caterpillars—Fiction.
2. Metamorphosis—Fiction] I. Title.
PZ7.B81698If 1983 [E] 82-15527

ISBN: 0-8050-1053-X (hardcover)
3 5 7 9 10 8 6 4
ISBN: 0-8050-1031-9 (paperback)
1 3 5 7 9 10 8 6 4 2

Henry Holt books are available at special discounts
for bulk purchases for sales promotions, premiums,
fund-raising, or educational use. Special editions
or book excerpts can also be created to specification.

For details, contact:

Special Sales Director
Henry Holt & Co., Inc.
115 West 18th Street
New York, New York 10011

First Owlet edition 1989
Printed in Italy

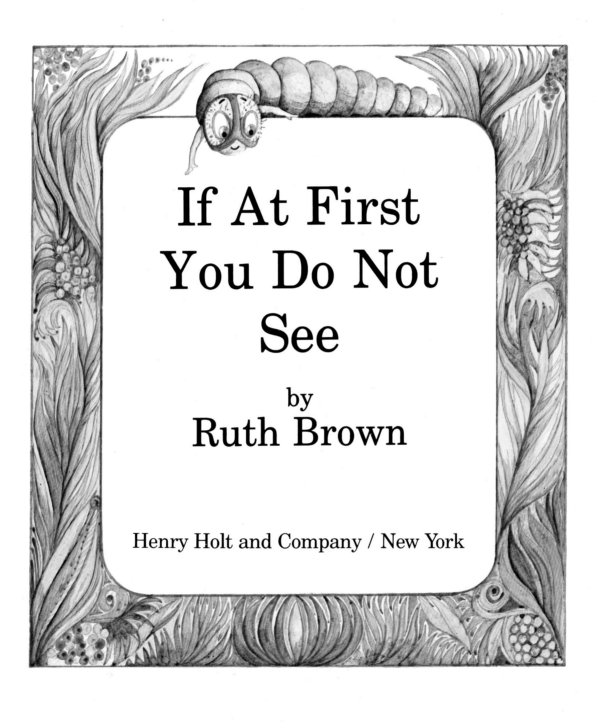

If At First You Do Not See

by
Ruth Brown

Henry Holt and Company / New York

"Now   stay here and eat those leaves,"
said the butterfly to her caterpillars.

"Ugh! How boring," said one caterpillar.
"I want something more appetizing. I'm leaving...."

"Oops! Sorry!" said the caterpillar as he crawled away.

"That looks a bit more juicy," said the caterpill

caterpillar. "Where are you?"

said a voice. "You're eating my hair!" "What?" said the

as he started to nibble. . . "Ouch! Get off!"

"Oh dear! I'm v-v-very sorry, sir."

And he very quickly climbed off the giant's face.

"Look at that lovely clump of grass . . .

"Wha-a-t?" said the caterpillar.

"Get off my nose, you nasty, green worm," a voice boomed.

I think I'll taste it," said the caterpillar.

saw the two funny men. "But I'm so hungry —

and I can't seem to find anything to eat."

"Mmm . . . delicious ice cream.

"Oh, I am so sorry," said the caterpillar as he

"Get off! Go away!" said two squeaky voices.

I'll have some of that," said the caterpillar.

— I don't like the looks of those two —

I think I'll get away from here . . . quickly!"

"Oh, look! A delicious mushroom!

But I'll just have a look to make sure it's safe.

That definitely looks good enough to eat.

Touch me and I'll feed you to my pretty bats."

"Aaaaaah!" screamed the caterpillar as he ran away.

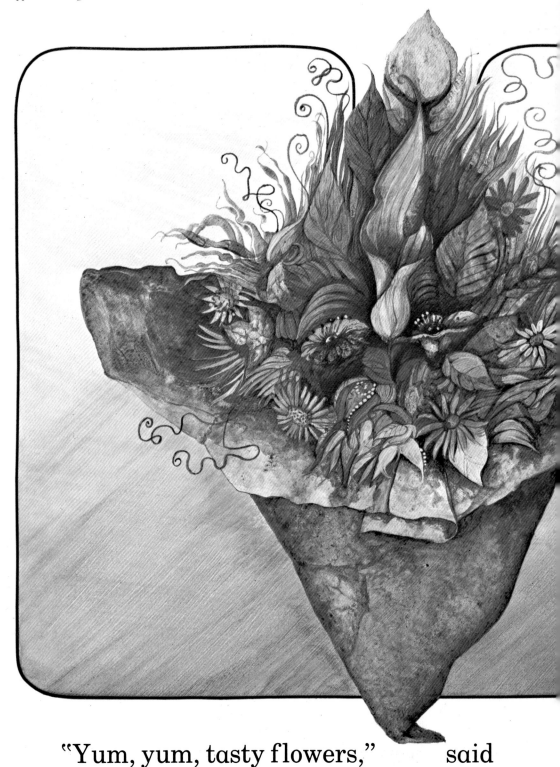

"Yum, yum, tasty flowers," said

you miserable little grub.

hissed a voice. "How dare you mistake me for stupid flowers,

the caterpillar. "Flowersssss, flowersssss,"

"Pardon me, I'm sure," said the caterpillar.

"You're too ugly to eat anyway," he shouted as he ran away.

"Oh! This is more like it – two juicy hamburgers!"

voice. "Yeah – go away," agreed a second.

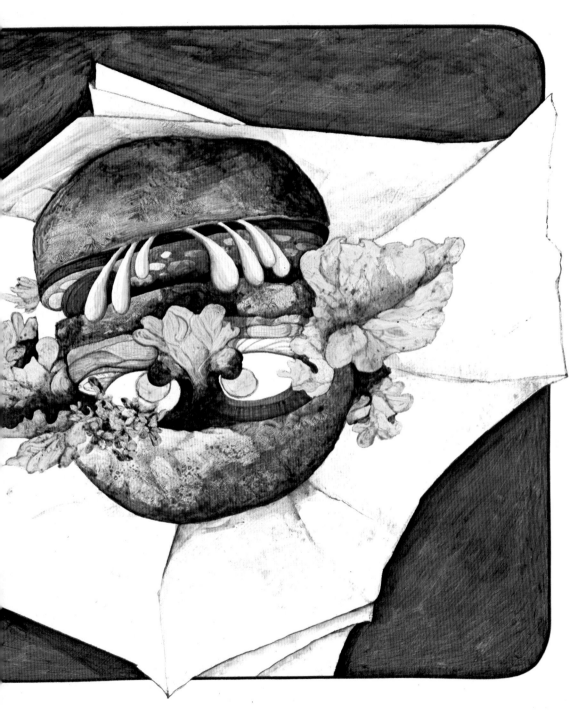

"Hey! Get off, you horrible little creepy-crawly," said a deep

said the caterpillar. "I'm hungry enough to eat both.'

But by this time . . .

the poor little caterpillar was fast, fast asleep.

"I'm starving, lonely, and exhausted," cried the

"What are you doing up there?" said a husky voice.

caterpillar. "I'll just have to rest in this straw."

"You poor little thing," said the scarecrow.

"I'll put you in my pocket. You'll be safe there."

It's just a field of leeks.

Aren't I a silly creature to be frightened of that!"

When he awoke he fell to the ground.

But wait a minute!

"I've got to get away from them as quickly as possible.

"Yikes! Look at those fierce looking men!" he cried.

that he had become a beautiful butterfly.

"Oh no! Another ugly monster! Hel-l-lp!"

"Who are you calling an ugly monster?

"Just a minute," said the creature.

The butterflies said good-bye to the scarecrow

They looked so beautiful and happy

and flew high up into the sky.